RAYMOND BRIGGS'

The Snowman ™

Ladybird Books

As soon as James got out
of bed he knew it would be
a magical day.

The best thing to do would be to make a SNOWMAN.

A big body and a big round head...

coal eyes,
a tangerine nose,
a hat and a scarf.

his snowman was *smiling*!

That night it was hard to sleep
so James got up to see his snowman.

This was magical...

his snowman was
walking towards
the house.

He explored the house with James.
The fridge was best — it was cold,
just how snowmen like it.

The snowman
tried
everything...

Then the snowman was outside,
running across the snow.
James went with him
and suddenly
they were...

walking in the air...

...looking far below...

...holding very tight...

and flying across the world.

When they landed,
the snowman led
James to some dark,
dark woods...

and there they
came upon the
most amazing
sight – all
the snowmen
and snow-women
of the world had
come for a party.

Next morning, James rushed out to see his snowman.

Had he been dreaming?

But he still had a scarf – his present from Father Christmas at the party.